# Buoy

## HOME AT SEA

BRUCE BALAN

ILLUSTRATIONS BY

### Raúl Colón

DELACORTE PRESS

*With heartfelt thanks to my editor, Lauri Hornik—B.B.*

...........................

PUBLISHED BY DELACORTE PRESS
Bantam Doubleday Dell Publishing Group, Inc.
1540 Broadway
New York, New York 10036

**Library of Congress Cataloging-in-Publication Data**
Balan, Bruce.
Buoy, home at sea / Bruce Balan ; illustrated by Raúl Colón.
p.   cm.
Summary: A series of stories about a buoy and some of the creatures and other natural elements that surround it in the sea.
ISBN 0-385-32539-8  [1. Ocean—fiction.  2. Buoys—Fiction.]
I. Colón, Raúl, ill.  II. Title.
PZ7.B1796Bu  1998
[Fic]—dc21  97-29233  CIP  AC

The text of this book is set in 11-point Dante.
*Book design by Susan Clark Dominguez*

Manufactured in the United States of America
June 1998
BVG  10 9 8 7 6 5 4 3 2 1

*For Paul, my uncle and friend* —B.B.

*In memory of Tito* —R.C.

# contents

# buoy

Buoy rolled lazily on the long low swell of the Sea. Buoy lived far from land; so far that only on the days when the Clouds raced against each other and the Wind seemed a bit angry, could Buoy just barely, ever so slightly, make out something to the east that was neither the Sea nor the Sky. But Buoy didn't mind at all. He loved the Sea and the Sky. He loved their blueness and wondered how it could be that his redness complemented them so perfectly.

1

Buoy had a bell. He thought that a bell was probably the most delightful thing to have in all the world. On warm, calm nights when the Wind had gone to bed early and every Star that ever was had come out to hear him, he would ring slowly and softly so that his music would have a chance to linger awhile by the Sea before beginning its journey to Heaven. And on cold foggy mornings, when the air was almost too sleepy to carry any noise at all, he would ring as boldly and solidly as he could, so that boats would have no question as to who he was and where he lived. And in times of the gravest danger, when the Wind went screaming in search of its past, and ships lost their way and wandered from the safe path to the west, he would ring loudly and urgently, to warn of the disaster that would occur if his call was not heeded.

Buoy also had a light. It sat on the top of his head. It was a red light, and Buoy could flash it. At first it had been very hard to remember how to do it just right. But now, Buoy had been doing it for so long that he didn't even have to think about it.

Flash flash flash; wait . . . wait . . . wait . . . wait. Flash flash flash; wait . . . wait . . . wait . . . wait. Flash flash flash.

Buoy never missed a flash or waited too long. And on the blackest of nights, when the Moon was visiting relatives far away, Buoy would concentrate as hard as he could to force his light through the darkness so that ships and boats would know that he was there to keep them on the safe path.

Buoy lived very far from land where people think it is lonely. But for Buoy, it was home.

# ship

Buoy could hear the ship coming when it was still a long way off.

Gull slept with his head under his wing.

Seal lay on her back. She liked the way the sunlight bounced on her belly.

"Ship coming," said Buoy.

No one moved.

"Ship coming," said Buoy again, and he rang his bell.

"Oh," said Seal.

"So . . . ?" said Gull.

"Don't you care?" asked Buoy.

5

"No," said Seal.

"You've seen one ship, you've seen 'em all," said Gull. "A ship's not like a hurricane or a herring, you know." He and Seal closed their eyes.

Buoy didn't say anything. He knew they wouldn't understand. He loved ships. A Ship-Coming was what he lived for. A Ship-Coming was *important*. He knew this the way he knew the sound of his bell. He knew, and he waited.

Slowly it approached from the north, its hugeness so small when it was far away. This one was a freighter; or so Buoy guessed, based on what Gull had once told him.

Closer and closer. Larger and larger. The ship seemed to grow out of the Sea. Buoy felt its thrumming deep inside his belly. He rolled with the swell. He flashed his light and rang his bell.

"Stay to the west," he whispered. "Stay to the west."

And the ship responded as if it heard. It altered course, leaving Buoy to port. But only by a few hundred feet.

Buoy looked up at the massive wall that slid past. *He* had kept it to the west. *He* had kept it safe from harm.

As the ship passed, its huge wake raced toward Buoy. He braced himself. He thought of warning Gull and Seal, but they had said they didn't want to be disturbed.

The wake hit with a splash. Buoy rocked noisily, throwing Seal into the Sea and knocking Gull off his perch. They spluttered and grumbled as they made their way back to their resting spots.

"Thanks for the warning, Buoy," Gull muttered.

"My pleasure," answered Buoy, still smiling because he had done his job. He had done it well.

# whale song

Porpoise was visiting. She looked toward the horizon. "I hear Whales," she said.

Porpoise was swimming next to Seal while Gull, as usual, stood on Buoy's head, leaning into the Wind.

"Are they close?" asked Buoy hopefully.

"Very," said Porpoise.

Everyone listened.

"I don't hear anything," said Gull.

"Shhh," said Seal.

Everyone listened.

"I still don't hear anything," said Gull grumpily.

"Shhh!" said Seal again.

Everyone listened. Gull shifted from one foot to the other.

"I hear them," whispered Seal.

Buoy listened hard. Faint tones swam through the blue Sea. Buoy heard the Whale song. It sounded very much like the song the Stars sang on crystal nights. But not so clear. And not so distant.

No one spoke. Except Gull, who harrumphed every few minutes.

They all listened.

It was a very old song. Though they could not understand it—Porpoise could pick out a few phrases here and there—they knew it was old. Older than Shark. Older than Rain. Even older than the Sea. Porpoise said it told of the first day of the Sea. And how the first Whale swam on that first day. And how the first Whale sang. And how the song created itself and everything else as well. There was much more, but it was too ancient for any of them ever to grasp.

The singing grew louder. Gray shapes appeared in the blue distance.

"I see them!" cried Buoy.

Closer they came. Moving the water with their magnificence. The sweep of their great flukes a metronome to their song.

When they were finally very close, Buoy spoke.

"Hello, Whales!" he called.

"Hello, Buoy," said one.

"Who do you sing to?" asked Buoy.

"We sing to the Stars," said the Whale.

"Why?"

"To let them know that we are here, and that we are watching still."

"What are you watching?" asked Buoy.

But the Whale had slid past, the dark blue closing behind
him as he went.

Flowing like the great ocean currents, the Whales had little time to stay and talk.

When their shapes had faded into the distance, and the last note of their song had quietly passed by on its long journey, Gull spoke.

"Can I talk now?" he said, still cranky.

"No," Buoy said gently.

And they all floated in silence, remembering.

# sailboat

Buoy let the Wind rock him gently. It was the laziest of days. The Sun was hot, and it made him sleepy. So sleepy that he didn't notice the small sailboat until it was quite close. There was no swell running; the Sea was thinking and couldn't be bothered to make waves today. Only the Breeze, which was very quiet so as not to disturb the Sea, wrinkled the smooth blueness a bit. The sailboat came slowly; white sails and deep green hull. It leaned over just a little with the light Wind. Several big people sat in the back. A small person sat in the front. His legs dangled over the edge and occasionally touched the water in a line of white bubbles. He sat leaning with his arms against the lifelines and looked out hard.

Buoy thought the small one was looking at him. The boat sailed closer. Buoy was sure the boy was looking right at him. Splashes came from the place where the bow kissed the Sea. The boat moved as if it were coasting down a long gentle hill.

The boy stared at Buoy. And just as the boat passed—so close that Buoy could have touched it if he had leaned over a little—the small one said gently, "Hello, Buoy." This, so quietly that Buoy wasn't even sure he had heard it. He was amazed. No person had ever spoken to him. They would often wave and bark at Seal, and either curse or screech at Gull, but they never spoke to Buoy.

By the time Buoy had recovered himself, the boat and the boy had sailed a good way off. Buoy rang his bell twice. And then a third time. He thought he saw the boy turn back . . . and wave.

# green flash

Sometimes—not always, just sometimes—when the Sea was calm and
the air was clear and the horizon was
so crisp and sharp and straight that
Seal and Gull and Buoy were almost
absolutely certain that the world was
flat; sometimes, at sunset, they would
wait for the Green Flash.

Seal would sit up eagerly while
Gull stood intently atop Buoy. All
would stare into the sunset, waiting
for the top edge of the great orange
ball to disappear below the horizon.
For at that moment, sometimes,

when everything was just right, the Sky would, for just half a second, glow green. And then it would be night.

Gull said it was a signal from the Sun to the Stars, telling them that it was time to come out. But Seal said it was when the Sun went down too close to the Sea and its yellow flames brushed against the Sea's blue waves. Gull said that was ridiculous and Seal said that it wasn't.

And occasionally Porpoise would come by and say that they were both wrong and that she knew what the Green Flash was but wasn't going to tell.

Buoy thought he might know. He had a hazy idea that there was another Buoy far away flashing in the night, and sometimes, with the help of the Sun, its light shone all the way across the Sea so that Buoy would know he wasn't alone. He never told Gull and Seal about this, but once he told Porpoise and she said that it wasn't very far from the truth. Buoy asked how far and where Truth was anyway. Was it to the west? The north? Porpoise smiled and said it didn't really matter.

But Buoy thought it did. So, whenever the time was right for the Green Flash, he flashed his own light. He flashed it as brightly as he could, hoping the other Buoy would see. Hoping the other Buoy would know he wasn't alone either.

# shark

Slowly he swam by. Not very often and not very fast. Dark in the blue water. He didn't like to talk. And he never spoke first.

"Hello, Shark," Buoy would say.

There would, of course, be no answer.

"Hello, Shark," he'd say again. Then he'd wait some more as Shark circled and circled.

But, as always on the second try, no reply.

And when he could wait no longer,

Buoy would clang his bell and shout, *"Hello, Shark!"*

When he finally spoke, Shark's voice was quiet, not cold. Mellow, not mean. And very, very patient.

"hello," Shark said, "hello, buoy. how is life?"

"It's wonderful!" answered Buoy. "And how is life for you?"

"hungry," Shark said. "hungry, and long."

Seal looked warily over Buoy's edge, down into the water at Shark circling around and around.

"There's no food here, Shark," said Seal. "Maybe you should look somewhere else."

"maybe," said Shark, slowly circling still. "maybe . . ."

Seal moved a little farther from the edge. She was not fond of Shark.

"You wouldn't hurt Seal, would you, Shark?" asked Buoy.

Shark slowed down just a little. There was a long pause. "i am as i was made," he said at last. Then he was silent again.

Buoy thought about this. He wasn't quite sure what it meant. Seal, however, was. She moved farther from the edge and closer to Buoy's bell.

Finally, after too long a time for Seal, and too short a time for Shark, Shark swam off—silent and mellow, slow and calm.

"Good-bye, Shark," Buoy said.

Shark never ever said good-bye.

# stars

Night came like a blanket of silence spread over the Sea. And woven through the blanket, Buoy's light— flashing, flashing into the black. Ships in the distance knew exactly where they were when they saw that flash. Ships at night were only lights far away—red or green, and white.

But some nights there were no ships, and Buoy and Gull and Seal and the Sea were left to themselves. Except for the Moon and the Stars.

The Moon, always changing, looked down with clear brightness, and Buoy felt its light deep in his heart. Then, in the silence, Buoy would wait for the Falling Stars.

He'd stare for hours into the black Sky. Sometimes there would be only one or two, or, on the unhappy nights, none. But sometimes there would be dozens. And as each Star raced across the Sky, Buoy could almost feel himself lifted a little out of the Sea, as if the Stars wanted him to follow.

"Where do they land?" asked Buoy.

"They don't land," said Gull authoritatively. "They miss the earth and keep going forever."

"No they don't," said Seal. "They fall on the other edge of the Sea. They make the water warm there. So warm that fish have to jump into the air to cool off."

"That's ridiculous!" said Gull. "Fish wouldn't do that even if the water *was* warm."

"What makes you so sure?" asked Seal. "You've never been there."

"Neither have you. But I could fly there if I wanted."

"Well, I could swim there. And I'd get there first."

"Oh yeah?"

"Yeah."

Back and forth they went. Until Seal was barking and Gull was screeching and neither was listening to what the other one was saying at all.

*Clang! Clang! Clang!*

Buoy rang his bell as loudly as he could. Startled, Gull and Seal stopped bickering. They looked at Buoy.

"Could we just watch the Stars for a while?" he said.

And then added, "Quietly."

And they did.

# below

Buoy stayed in one spot on the Sea. Because below him, he had a tail of chain that stretched down and down and down and down. Seal could not swim that far down. Nor could Porpoise. Shark didn't even respond when Buoy asked him to try.

But Buoy knew that his chain went all the way to the floor of the Sea. And though he couldn't quite explain how he did it, he could sometimes follow the chain all the way down.

This usually happened when he was drifting off for a nap. On hot days, with the waves rolling him gently and no ships in sight, he would sometimes begin to feel drowsy. Back and forth he'd rock. And as he sank into sleep, his spirit would settle, slowly, beneath the waves. And there, he would see . . .

The sea grass hanging below him, swaying back and forth as if forever beckoning to the schools of tiny fish that swam past. The sunlight creating a sparkling roof of illuminated waves above.

Then down the chain. To where the water grew cold. And much larger fish swam by. And Shark ate them. There was no yellow here. No orange. No red.

Then down the chain. To where the light became dim. And green could not dive this deep. Only very dark blue.

Then down the chain. To where there was no color at all. But strange creatures lived here. Creatures that glowed in the darkness.

Then down the chain. To the seabed. And there, rooted in the depth of the Sea, Buoy felt a humming. A hum that seemed to come from deeper than the Sea. It reminded him somehow of the song of the Whales. But he did not hear this song. He felt it. It seemed to be part of who he was. He did not understand that it was *he* who was a part of the *song*.

# concert

Buoy spun slowly—around and around—scanning the horizon.

No Whales.

"I wish I could sing," he muttered.

No one said anything.

"I wish I could sing," he said again, and then added, "like the Whales."

Gull rolled his eyes, shook his head, and was about to say something when Seal interrupted.

"You sing in your own way, Buoy," she said. "You have your bell."

The thought didn't cheer Buoy. He loved his bell. He loved the fine clear

note it made. But it was only *one* note. And *he* was the only one who played it.

"It's not the same," he replied sullenly. "The Whales sing together. But there are no other Buoys to play with me."

"We'll help," Seal offered.

"Who's we?" Gull asked.

Buoy brightened. "Really?"

"Yes." Seal sat up. "I'll show you. Ring your bell every time I tap my flipper."

Seal began tapping, and Buoy tried to follow the rhythm.

*Clang, cla-clang . . . Clang, clang.*

*Clang, cla-clang . . . Clang, clang.*

Then Seal turned to Gull. "You give a flap and a screech to the beat of my tail."

"I'm not having any part of this—" Gull began.

"Start *now*," Seal said with a severe look.

*Flap-screech, flap-screech . . . flap-screech, flap-screech.*

Seal continued tapping and began adding a few barks of her own.

They practiced all afternoon. At first their song sounded awful, but slowly they improved. Buoy learned to keep the rhythm all by himself. Seal produced different notes by drumming on various parts of Buoy's body. Gull forgot that he wasn't having a good time.

The Sun sank low. Still they played on. The Stars came out to listen, but the musicians didn't notice. Each was lost in the music they were creating together.

Finally, knowing deep down that it was just the right moment, they ended their song with a magnificent finale of barks, screeches, and clangs.

Silence.

And then . . . splashes, whistles, and hoots!

The three musicians opened their eyes. An audience had gathered. Porpoise was there, as well as several sea lions, three pelicans, a turtle, and dozens of fish.

"Bravo!" they cried.

Gull bowed. Seal smiled shyly. Buoy scanned the distant horizon.

"Encore!" the crowd demanded.

Buoy saw what he had hoped to see. He smiled too as Seal counted out the beginning of their next song. Seal nodded toward him, and he rang his bell to the beat. Gull joined in. And as they played, Buoy watched the great tails of several Whales slap the surface three times each and then disappear joyfully beneath the waves.

# storm

The night was always blackest during a storm, and a storm was always meanest at night. The Wind tore the Sea, picking up bits, flinging them about, and turning them into foam. The distant Clouds that had tumbled over each other at twilight now roared overhead, mostly invisible in the darkness, but adding their thunderous yell to the Wind's scream.

Buoy looked into the blackness and thought how harsh the world was during a storm. He was not frightened; he had seen many storms, and they did him no harm. But he knew that storms could be dangerous to other creatures. And to ships.

Buoy *enjoyed* the storm a little. The waves tried to drag him along as they roared past, but he stayed right where he was anchored. He would watch each wave as it rushed away toward the east, and then turn to face the next one as it approached, frothing with impatience.

Then he spotted the boat. It was a small boat, and Buoy knew immediately that something was wrong. Its sails were ripped and shredded. Out of control, it was being pushed sideways by the waves. A man and a woman and a tiny child huddled under the dodger as the fierce Wind tore at the remaining strips of canvas that hung from the mast. They did not see Buoy. Waves picked the boat up and hurled it wildly, nearly capsizing it. Buoy could tell there must already be a great deal of water in the boat because it floated low.

As the boat came closer, Buoy gave his bell a mighty ring and flashed his light as brightly as he could. The woman looked up, grabbed the man's arm, and pointed toward Buoy. Quickly the man made his way to the front of the boat, grabbed a line, and tied it to the bow. The little boat was moving fast. They would have only one chance.

As the boat came close, Buoy leaned. He leaned with all the energy he had. With all of his will, he leaned toward the man's outstretched hand. Buoy leaned until he could lean no farther. And just as he felt himself starting to roll back, the man's fingers stretched an extra inch and grabbed Buoy's mooring ring. The man quickly attached the rope

and then returned to the stern, where the woman was already bailing the water out.

When it looked as though they would not sink, the man and woman wrapped a blanket around their child and themselves. They stayed there all night, huddled on the floor of the boat, shivering against the cold Wind. Meanwhile, Buoy kept a watchful eye on them and tried as best he could to block the iciest of the storm's blasts and the worst of the Sea's waves.

In the morning the storm had blown itself away, and Buoy and the little boat bobbed on the Sea, which was still slightly upset from the night's terror. The man, the woman, and the child unfolded themselves from their embrace and looked around, amazed that this sunny spot was the same one that had been so frightening only a few hours before.

Throughout the morning the man and the woman worked on the boat's outboard motor. The child helped by finding misplaced tools and picking up lost screws. Gull, thinking the family might be hungry, dropped a small fish into the boat. Though they laughed, they didn't eat it and instead threw it over the side. Seal swam about, playing peekaboo with the little one.

After many, many hours, with a groan and then a splutter, the motor came to life. The woman took the helm, and the man went to the bow. He carefully untied the line that had secured them through the long night. And, as he gently pushed the boat away, he whispered, "Thank you."

# travelers

An egg carton, broken in half, floated by. It had been in the Sea for a very long time. Buoy could tell because it was worn and tired looking, and green sea grass hung from its bottom, delicately dancing in the currents.

"Hello, Buoy." Small voices came up from the carton. "Hello!"

Buoy looked down. "Hello, crabs," he said. "Where are you going?"

"To see the world, Buoy. We're taking our ship and going to see the world."

"Wonderful," replied Buoy. "Do you know how to get there? Do you know which way to go?"

"Oh no! No, no, no!" cried the tiny crabs as they scurried over and under each other. "Do you?"

"I don't," said Gull.

"Nor I," said Seal.

"Perhaps it's across the Sea," Buoy suggested.

"The Sea? The Sea! Where is the Sea?" The crabs could barely keep themselves from falling over the edge of their egg carton as they clamored and crowded and crawled about.

Seal looked at Gull. Gull rolled his eyes, then flew away, groaning to himself.

Buoy thought for a moment. "Keep going," he said. "I think you're heading in exactly the right direction."

The crabs scrambled to the front of their fragile ship. They peered over the edge, out across the never-ending blue.

"Ohhh," they whispered.

Their egg carton bobbed along, and Seal smiled.

Gull circled overhead, keeping an eye out for Shark. Buoy rang his bell gently and watched the travelers sail off in search of the world.

Voices, small and eager, floated back across the Wind. "Good-bye, Seal. Good-bye, Gull. Good-bye, Buoy."

"Good-bye, crabs," they replied. "Good luck."

Buoy rang his bell all night long that night, even though there was no storm and it was not foggy. Though the crabs were far away, he thought maybe they could still hear him through the damp blackness. He thought they would probably like that.

# clouds

"It's a herring," Gull said with authority. "What else could it be?"

"I think it looks like a crab," said Seal.

"You're crazy," argued Gull. "It's a herring. And that one there is a fishing boat."

"No, it's not. It's a rock by the shore, perfect for sunning oneself on."

"Are you blind?" Gull asked. "It's a fishing boat! Don't you see the nets? And the man tossing bait over the stern?"

"It's a sunning rock," Seal insisted.

"You've been lying with your head too close to that bell!" Gull grumbled.

"What do you think, Buoy?" Seal asked.

Buoy looked up at the jumbly masses of white as they floated high in the pale blue Sky.

"I think they're having fun," he said.

"Who?" Gull asked, quite annoyed. *He* wasn't having fun.

"The Clouds," Buoy answered. "See how they roll around and pile on top of each other? They're playing."

Gull flew off his perch and landed next to Seal. He looked up at Buoy and gave his wings an impatient flap.

"But who's right? Is that a herring or a crab?" he demanded. "And is that one a fishing boat or a rock?"

Buoy stared at the great billowing Clouds. Gull paced. Seal laid her head back down and closed her eyes. Finally Buoy spoke.

"Well, Gull, that one looks like you. And the other one
looks like Seal."

"Ohhh!" Gull flew up to his perch and turned his back on
the Clouds. "Why do I bother!"

"What's the matter? What did I say?" Buoy asked, surprised.

"Nothing, Buoy," Seal said without raising her head. She
smiled. "Just the truth, that's all."

# slick

It was interesting to see, but it felt wrong. A yellow glow to the north. It wasn't the Moon. And it wasn't ships' lights. It wasn't Stars either, though Seal suggested that maybe a Star had fallen a little way away. Buoy didn't think so. Whatever it was, it lit up the night sky and changed it to an uncomfortable orange, sometimes flickering green and then blue or red or white.

"I don't like it," said Gull.

Neither did Buoy.

The next morning Buoy felt sticky. He felt sluggish and slow. He opened his eyes and looked around. The Sun was just beginning to light up the Sea. But where was the blue?

As far as Buoy could see, the Sea was black. Shining black and gray. Buoy could feel the blackness cling to him as he rolled with the low swell. The black even seemed to be trying to stop the swell. It seemed to be trying to smother anything that wasn't black.

"Gull! Seal! Wake up!" Buoy called.

"What's the mat— Oh!" said Seal.

"Will you keep the racket down," grouched Gull. "It's too early for all this yell— Oh . . . Oh! Oil!"

"What?" asked Buoy. "What is it?"

"Oil," echoed Seal. "It's oil, Buoy."

"That's what we saw last night," said Gull. "A ship must have caught fire and spilled all this."

They sat in silence for a while and looked across the sad

blackness toward the place where they had seen the strange light the night before.

"Seal," Gull said suddenly, "we have to go."

"I know," she said.

"What?" cried Buoy. "You can't leave me here in the middle of all this . . . oil!"

"We have to, Buoy," said Seal. "We're sorry, but we must. Gull can't fish through the oil. If it gets on him he won't be able to fly. And I can only swim in it for so long. It's poison."

"Will you come back?" Buoy asked softly.

"Of course we will. As soon as it's safe."

And then they left, Seal swimming underwater for as long as she could and Gull slowly circling above her to make sure she was all right.

Buoy watched them go. Straining to see Seal's head pop up through the murky goo, he shuddered to think of

# birthday

Many days passed, and Seal and Gull finally returned. As did the blue of the Sea.

Buoy awoke one morning to feel something tugging on him.

"Seal! Gull! Wake up! Something's got me!"

Seal looked up sleepily. "Hmmm?"

Gull flapped his wings twice in irritation. "Keep quiet, Buoy. It's early."

"No, no!" cried Buoy. "Something's got me!"

Gull and Seal opened their eyes again, looked around, and smiled.

the blackness actually touching his friend.

When he could see them no longer he turned and looked around. He noticed a thin wisp of smoke rising in the north. He was very sad. He felt sorry for himself because he was alone. He felt sorry for Gull and Seal because they had to leave their home. But mostly, as he looked out over the thick black ooze, he felt sorry for the Sea. Because the Sea had nowhere to go.

"Don't worry, Buoy." Seal laughed. "I think *you've* got *it*."

"What?" cried Buoy, still very nervous. "What have I got?"

Gull grabbed the something and pulled it away from Buoy's light, where it had tangled itself during the night. He flew down next to Seal with the thing flying from his beak.

Buoy looked at it. Awe filled his heart. It was so beautiful! Red, just as he was. With a white ribbon curling gracefully below. And it flew—bobbing and bouncing in the air, just as he bobbed and bounced on the Sea.

"What is it?" Buoy asked, almost breathless with wonder.

Gull held the ribbon with his feet so he could speak. "It's a balloon, Buoy."

"There's writing on it, Gull," said Seal. "What does it say?"

Gull looked hard at the balloon, and he thought hard too. "It says, 'Hap . . . py Bir . . . th . . . day. Happy Birthday!'"

"*Thank you!*" Buoy practically exploded. Gull, surprised, jumped back and almost lost his hold on the balloon. "You remembered my birthday!" exclaimed Buoy. "What wonderful friends you are. I didn't even know it *was* my birthday!"

"But Buoy," Seal began, "it wasn't—"

"Hrmph!" Gull shushed Seal. "We're glad you like it," he said to Buoy.

"I do. Yes, I do," said Buoy. "Please, Gull, put it back on my light for me."

Gull flew up and carefully tied the balloon to Buoy's light. And there it stayed for many, many days.

# new paint

Men came in a big boat and pulled Buoy up out of the water with a crane. Gull flew off, complaining with loud screeches. No one took notice. Seal floated a little bit away, wondering what was going on.

The men looked at Buoy very carefully. They looked at his light and at his bell. They scraped off the long sea grass that hung from his bottom. They rubbed him with rough brushes wherever he was rusty, and they replaced one of the wires that ran to his light. Then they painted him. Red.

Bright, glossy red. A brighter red than Buoy could ever remember being. And when he was dry, they gently lowered him back into the Sea.

When the men left, Seal jumped up and settled back into her accustomed place. She sniffed once at the new paint and then laid her head down and closed her eyes.

Gull flew down and landed on his perch on Buoy's head. His feet slipped a little on the slick finish, and he cast his eyes critically over Buoy.

"You're different," said Gull.

"Not really," said Buoy. "I just look different."

"Hmmm," said Gull thoughtfully. "All right then."

# pup

"Seal, you're getting fat," said Buoy.

Gull snickered. Seal smiled.

"I'm not getting fat," said Seal.

"Well . . . plump then," Buoy said, trying to be polite. "You're getting a little bit plump."

Gull guffawed. Seal smiled again.

"That's not what I meant," she said.

"Well, what did you mean?" asked Buoy, a bit irritated at Gull's laugh.

Gull couldn't stand it any longer. "She's not fat, you bell-brain, she's pregnant!"

"Pregnant? Wow," said Buoy. "You mean you're going to have a pup?"

"Yes," said Seal. And she smiled a third time.

Many days passed, and then one morning Seal swam away toward the east.

More days passed. And more. Far too many for Buoy. He was lonely without Seal.

Gull would fly east every so often and bring back reports.

"Any day now."

"It'll be soon."

"Tomorrow. Count on it."

"I feel it in my feathers. Tomorrow for sure."

"Yep, tomorrow is the day. As sure as there's fish in the Sea."

And finally . . .

"It's a girl!"

More days passed. Buoy couldn't stand it!

"When are they coming?" he'd cry, and then he'd beg Gull to fly east and check on them just one more time.

At last Seal came back. With her she had her newborn pup, short and round and big-eyed and wondering.

"Daughter," Seal said, "this is Buoy."

"Hello, Buoy. Hello."

"Nice to meet you," said Buoy.

"Yes, it is," said the pup. Then she looked at him closely. "Who are you?" she asked.

"I'm Buoy," Buoy answered.

"What's a *buoy*?" asked the pup.

"Well," said Buoy, "I'm someone to climb on for rest. I'll protect you from Shark. And I'm someone to talk to and look at the Moon with. And I'm here all the time. And I'll tell you about ships and how I keep them safe with my

light. And about the Green Flash and the Whales' song. And we can watch Falling Stars together. And talk to Porpoise. I'll ring my bell for you. And I'll rock you to sleep every night."

The pup looked up at Seal, wondering what Buoy was talking about.

Seal jumped up onto Buoy. "He's one of the family," she said. "This is our home."

Buoy beamed. He looked at the new pup splashing at his side. At Seal lying on her back, leaning warmly against him. At Gull flying overhead, keeping an eye out for Shark. At the white Clouds playing charades in the blue Sky. He looked at the Sea. Her long low swells approaching so gracefully, so smoothly. A constant greeting he knew so well. The Sea in which he lived. In which they all lived.

*Yes,* he thought, *this is home.*

# about the author

BRUCE BALAN is an avid sailor and certified scuba diver. He met Buoy one night while boating near Point Fermin, California, with his uncle Paul.

Born in Long Beach, California, Bruce Balan graduated from San Francisco State University. He has worked as a videotape engineer, plumber, nanny, sous-chef, computer software designer, and writing instructor, among other jobs. Currently a full-time writer, he has published several picture books and a middle-grade mystery series. He and his wife, Dana, live in Los Altos, California.

# about the illustrator

RAÚL COLÓN is an acclaimed illustrator whose work has appeared on book jackets and in numerous magazines and newspapers. He has illustrated several picture books, receiving for them gold and silver medals from the Society of Illustrators and a *New York Times* Best Illustrated Book of the Year honor. Though a native New Yorker, he has lived in Puerto Rico, where he studied commercial art, and in Florida, where he worked for ten years as an animator, puppeteer, and set designer at an educational television center. Raúl Colón currently lives in New City, New York, with his wife and two children.